*Other Books
by Natalie Babbitt*

THE SEARCH FOR DELICIOUS
GOODY HALL

To Maureen
from Natalie Babbit

April 28, 1978

Knee-Knock Rise

STORY AND PICTURES BY

NATALIE BABBITT

CAMELOT BOOKS/PUBLISHED BY AVON

Dr. Donald B. Potter, Professor of Geology at Hamilton College, assures me that the phenomenon at the top of Kneeknock Rise, while somewhat improbable, is nevertheless not impossible. Dr. Thomas E. Colby III, folklorist and Professor of German at Hamilton, has helped me choose the charms and fetishes that are found in use at Instep. My thanks to both these patient gentlemen. I would also like to thank Percy Townsend, who graciously consented to pose for the pivotal role of Sweetheart.

AVON BOOKS
A division of
The Hearst Corporation
959 Eighth Avenue
New York, New York 10019

First Camelot Printing, February, 1974.
Third Printing

CAMELOT TRADEMARK REG. U.S. PAT. OFF.
AND IN OTHER COUNTRIES,
MARCA REGISTRADA, HECHO EN U.S.A.

Printed in the U.S.A.

This book is for *Alice,*
who spent the last days of a long
and happy life serving as a model,
in every particular, for *Annabelle*

*Facts are the barren branches
on which we hang the dear, obscuring
foliage of our dreams*

THE MAMMOTH MOUNTAINS WERE not really mountains at all. No glaciers creased their rocky, weed-strewn slopes, no eagles screamed above their modest summits. An hour or so would bring you to the top, puffing a little, perhaps, but not exhausted, and the view, once you were there, was hardly worth the climb. Nevertheless, the people who lived there were extremely proud of the mountains, for they were the only point of interest in a countryside that neither rolled nor dipped but lay as flat as if it had been knocked unconscious.

Because of this pride of the people's, you were well advised, on passing through, to remember the famous and somewhat true story of an early visitor who rashly remarked that anyone who could call those molehills mountains had to be either a blindman or a fool. It was suggested to him that he was already a fool himself and in grave danger of becoming a blindman on the instant. So, we are told, he wisely thought better of it, looked again, and said, "I see that I was mistaken. No mere mole could have made those mounds. They must have been the work of a mammoth!" The people were satisfied, the visitor escaped unharmed, and the mountains were christened.

However, the Mammoth Mountains had far more to offer than pride of ownership and rest for the eye that was weary of level plains. One of the mounds was different from its brothers, rockier, taller, and decidedly more cliff-like, with steeper sides and fewer softening trees, and its crest was forever shrouded in a little cloud of mist. Here lay the heart of the mountains' charm; here, like Eve's forbidden fruit, dwelt their mystery, for good or evil. For from somewhere in that mist, on stormy nights when the rain drove harsh and cold, an undiscovered creature would lift its voice and moan. It moaned like a lonely demon, like a mad, despairing animal, like a huge and anguished something chained forever to its own great tragic disappointments.

Nobody knew what it was that lived high up in the mist. As far back as memory could grope, no one had climbed the cliff to see. The creature had mourned there for a thousand years, in isolation so splendid, and with sorrows so infinitely greater than any of their own, that the people were struck with awe and respect. Therefore, climbing the cliff was something they simply did not do, and curious children were early and easily discouraged from trying by long and grisly tales which told what might well happen if they did.

From time to time, in the land below the cliff, strange things in fact did happen. A straying sheep would be found slaughtered, a pail of milk would sour, a chimney would unreasonably topple. These things were considered by some to be the work of the creature on the cliff, while others refused to believe that it ever left its misty nest. But they all had their favorite charms against it, and to all of them the cliff was the grandest, most terrible thing in the world. They trembled over it, whispered about it, and fed their hearts to bursting with gleeful terrors. It was frightful and fine and it belonged to them. They called it Kneeknock Rise.

❧❧

At the foot of Kneeknock Rise, on its southern side, stood a village appropriately called Instep. Instep was closer to the Rise than any other village and was therefore exalted among villages, a sort of Mecca where you could go from time to time and renew yourself with reports of the latest storm, fatten your store of descriptions that strove endlessly to define once and for all the chilling sounds that wound down from the clifftop, and go home again to enjoy in your own village the celebrity you deserved —until someone else went off and returned with newer reports. Instep was famous in that flat and hungry land and the people who lived in Instep, made smug and rich by tourists and privilege, had fallen into the custom of flinging their gates wide, once a year, and inviting everyone for miles around to come to a Fair. The Fair was always held in the autumn, when storms were fierce and frequent, and was a gesture of generosity on the part of Instep whereby its inhabitants could say, "Come and eat and dance; be entertained and spend your money; and—hear the Megrimum for yourselves." For this was the name they had come to use when speaking of the mournful creature that lived at the top of Kneeknock Rise.

"Now, don't forget!" said Egan's mother for the twentieth time. "When you get to Instep, go directly to your Uncle Anson's house. Don't go wandering about the shops. Your Aunt Gertrude will worry if you're not there by six, and she's been worried enough since Ott disappeared."

"If Aunt Gertrude is as fussy as you say, no wonder Uncle Ott keeps running off," said Egan, pulling crossly at his new collar. "I wish I could stay with someone else."

"Nonsense!" said his mother. "If you're going to the Instep Fair, of course you must stay with your aunt and uncle. Anyway, Gertrude isn't exactly fussy. She's just nervous. Who wouldn't be nervous, living at the bottom of the Rise? I don't see how they stand it all year round. It's very good of Gertrude and Anson to look after Ott, seeing as he's never done a thing but read his books and write all those

8

verses. And then, too, he's sick so often. Colds and wheezing. It can't be easy for them, even if he *is* your Uncle Anson's only brother." She walked around her son, eyeing him critically, and brushed a bit of lint from his shoulder. "Now, Egan, do be polite to Gertrude and Anson. They're so pleased you're coming to the Fair, and it will be a real treat for your Cousin Ada. Little Ada! Why, I haven't seen her since she was a baby!"

❧❦

Egan rode across the countryside to Instep with his father's friend, the chandler, who was taking a load of fragrant new candles to sell at the Fair. It was forty miles from home to the gates of Instep, a long, tiresome ride on the hard seat of a bulky cart drawn by a very resentful mule the chandler called Frieda. The mule sometimes walked so slowly that you were sure she had fallen asleep, but she could also decide, quite suddenly and without warning, to break into a gallop. Every time this happened, Egan and the chandler would fall over backwards into the straw-packed candles behind them and then have to struggle upright, while the cart hurtled crazily down the road, and yell at Frieda until they were hoarse. The mule would stop eventually, gasping and glaring as if it were all their fault, and then the whole process would begin over again.

It was just after one of the galloping episodes that the chandler suddenly put his hand on Egan's arm and pointed. "There they are!" he said excitedly. "And there *it* is!" Along the level horizon, sure enough, a row of dark bumps had appeared. One of the bumps, narrower and straighter than the others, rose up in the middle of the row, crowned by a shred of mist that shimmered in the clear autumn sunshine.

"Is that it?" asked Egan in a low voice, squinting at the distant cliff. "I've never seen it before."

"That's it!" whispered the chandler. "I've seen it fifty times, but it always makes me shiver. It's a grand sight, grander close up." He prodded the dawdling mule impatiently with his driving stick. "Hurry up, Frieda, can't you?" he cried. "Get a move on!" Then his voice dropped again and he murmured, "That's it, all right. That's Kneeknock Rise."

❧

When Egan arrived at last, he was tired and dusty and somehow resentful of the somber thrust of the cliff that had loomed larger and larger as the cart jolted over the fields toward Instep. It was too big, he decided; too proud. He scowled at it jealously. And the first sight of his Uncle Anson's house did nothing to improve his mood. A little girl was sitting on the wall that enclosed the small house and yard, and she studied him critically as he walked along the road to the gate. She was a skinny little girl with red hair strained back into one long pigtail and she was covered with scratches. She was cuddling something in her arms and he saw as he came up that it was a large, rust-colored cat.

"You're Egan," the little girl informed him.

"I know," he said.

"Say hello to Sweetheart," she commanded, and she thrust the cat forward. It was a very well-fed cat, battle-scarred and insolent, and it stared at Egan coldly out of narrowed yellow eyes, the tip of its tail switching slowly back and forth. Then suddenly it reached out a claw and scratched him across the cheek.

"Ow!" yelled Egan. "Quit that!"

The cat hissed at him, twisted neatly out of the small hands that held it, and lounged off down the road.

"For goodness' sake," said Egan, touching his wound tenderly. "What a terrible cat!"

"Sweetheart is the loveliest cat in the world," said the little girl firmly. "He just doesn't like you. I don't like you, either. I'm Ada and I guess we're cousins."

"I guess so," said Egan. He looked at Ada with despair.

"You certainly are a mess," said Ada contemptuously. "How come you're all covered with straw?" Then she grabbed his arm with her sharp little fingers and pointed. "Look there! You never saw that before, did you? I see it every day. It practically belongs to me. Uncle Ott ran off up there and the Megrimum ate him." She smiled rapturously and pointed again.

Egan looked up just as the sun dropped down behind the mountains. A long shadow fell across the house and yard from beyond the wall, where the green and purple face of the rocky hillside rose into the evening sky. It was huge and silent and cold as a gravestone. As he stared, the mist at the top went blood-red in the sunset.

"I guess you're pretty scared," suggested Ada hopefully.

"Don't be silly," said Egan. "I'm not afraid of anything." But he shuddered just the same.

"Here's Egan, Mother," said Ada when she had pulled him into the house. "Here he is at last. Isn't he a mess? Sweetheart scratched him." She giggled and put the end of her pigtail into her mouth.

Aunt Gertrude put aside a bit of sewing and came forward. She was as thin as her daughter and her narrow face was fringed with pale yellow hair. "Welcome to Instep, Egan," she said. "Dear me! You look exactly like your father! I never could understand how my own sister could marry such a man. So big and cheerful and noisy. I do hope you won't be noisy. You're awfully large for your age, aren't you? Dear me! You really do look just like him. And aren't you dusty! Heavens, look at that scratch. Whatever shall we do about Sweetheart? Such a disagreeable cat!" Still talking, she led him away to a small room at the back of the house.

Egan felt better when he saw the room. There was a cot against one wall, with pillows and a pile of worn and comfortable quilts. The corners of the room were cluttered with little heaps of books and papers, and on a large table, besides the usual pitcher and bowl, there were quills and ink and an old pipe. The cloth on the table was stained with blots and pen scratches. It was all very untidy and interesting.

"This will be your room, Egan," said his aunt. "You'd better wash yourself. I do hope you're not feeling too bad after your trip?"

"I'm feeling fine, Aunt Gertrude."

"What a brave, good boy!" she exclaimed. "Of course you're feeling wretched and exhausted. Why don't you lie down? No, you'd better wash first. This is Ott's room, you know—did you know he's disappeared again?"

"My mother told me," said Egan.

"Well, I'm sure I don't know what to do," said Aunt Gertrude, sitting down on the cot and wringing her hands. "Ott's been away for three days, and just before the Fair, too. Not that it isn't easier without him, you know, but he's a good man in his way, a gentle man, and I'm so afraid he may have gone—up there. That would have been a dreadfully foolish thing to do!" She dabbed at her eyes with the hem of her apron. Egan watched her and decided that she was enjoying the excitement very much, in spite of her nervous manner.

"You're a bright and clever boy, I can see that," she said, and Egan made another decision: he was going to like Aunt Gertrude. "Yes," she went on, "you're intelligent. You get that from our side of the family. Well, wash up and then take a rest. I'll try to keep Ada quiet, but she's such a stubborn child. I'm sure I don't know what to do with her." She stood up— and there was a sharp yelp from under the cot.

Aunt Gertrude shrieked and jumped aside. "Good heavens! Ott! Is that you, Ott? What are you doing under there?" She went down on elbows and knees and peered under the cot while Egan waited, round-eyed. "It's only Annabelle," announced Aunt Gertrude in a normal tone. "I thought it might be Ott, but it's only Annabelle." She stood up and brushed the dust from her elbows. "Poor old Annabelle. She loved him so. How could he have gone away and left her? Come, Annabelle! Come out now, dear. I'm sorry I stepped on you. Well, she won't come out. I hope you don't mind, Egan. She seems to want to stay there." And Aunt Gertrude left the room and closed the door behind her.

᠑᠍᠊

Egan stood quite still in the middle of the little room and wondered, somewhat nervously, who —or what—this Annabelle might be. He waited, hoping that something would happen. He had the distinct feeling that Annabelle was waiting, too. However, after a few minutes, the sound of gentle snoring filled the room. Annabelle had stopped waiting and had obviously gone to sleep. "It ought to be safe to look now, anyway," he said to himself, and he crouched down and peered under the cot. In the dusty gloom that hung there, the special cozy gloom that keeps to itself under every bed, he saw what at first appeared to be the round stomach and tapering legs of a whiter-than-average pig. "Strange to keep a pig indoors," he thought, and then, "But it seems too frazzy, somehow, to be a pig. Perhaps it's some kind of animal I've never seen before." He pondered the dim white shape for a moment and then said, experimentally, "Annabelle?" The snoring stopped at once. In its place came a soft thump-thump and then silence.

"Well, there's only one thing to do," said Egan. "I'll have to move the cot." He stood up and dragged the cot carefully away from the wall and out into the middle of the room. There, exposed at last to the blue and peaceful twilight, lay Annabelle—Annabelle who had dearly loved his Uncle Ott but had been left behind. She was a dog—a dog with graceful white feet and ankles, a thick white chest, and a bulging stomach that hinted pink where the hairs were sparse and coarse. Across her back and hips were large, irregular brown spots, and her head, which was really too small for her body, wore several shades of brown that arched over her eyes, giving her a surprised and interested expression. Around her neck a thick roll of extra flesh fanned out soft fur into a deep, inviting ruffle and her ears drooped like rich brown velvet triangles. She was old and fat and beautiful and Egan was instantly enchanted. "Hello, you good old Annabelle," he said, and dropped to his knees to pat her. She looked up at him, her brown eyes sad and misty, and then as if she had said to herself, "Well, well, perhaps . . ." her eyes cleared and seemed to smile. She rolled heavily onto her broad, flat back and, four legs akimbo, presented the meager hairs of her stomach for scratching. Egan scratched and after a moment she lifted her head awkwardly and licked him on the knee. They were friends.

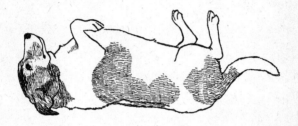

Uncle Anson came home not long after, at suppertime, with a large package under his arm. "I've done it, Gertrude," he said solemnly to his wife. "It's finished. It will be the wonder of the Fair."

"Say hello to Egan," said Aunt Gertrude.

"Hello, Nephew," said Uncle Anson. "Welcome to Instep. Gather round, everyone. Come and see what I have here."

Ada was sitting on the floor in a corner of the room, playing with Sweetheart. "It's just another clock," she guessed without interest. "I'll see it later."

"Just another clock?" cried Uncle Anson in an anguished tone. "No, indeed, not just another clock. *The* clock. The only one of its kind in the world."

Egan came to the table eagerly. "My mother told me to be sure and see the clocks you make, but there's not a single one in the house," he said, watching as Uncle Anson opened the package tenderly.

"He keeps them all at the shop now," said Aunt Gertrude. "We used to have his clocks all over everywhere, but I can't stand it any more. All they do is sit there and tick you away into old age and rheumatism. And the striking! Bong! Time to get up. Bong! Time to do the washing. Bong! Time for lunch—and so on and so on till you're half crazy. Oh, but Anson!" she gasped as the paper fell away at last, "that's a very beautiful clock indeed!"

Uncle Anson, having unveiled his masterpiece, lifted it and hung it from a peg on the wall. Then he stepped back dramatically and sighed. The clock *was* handsome. It looked like a big figure 8 set against a rectangular back and wreathed with twining wooden twigs and leaves. The lower half of the 8 was the clock face itself, but the upper half was a cleverly carved bird's nest containing a large wooden egg, while two more eggs did for the weights. It was all fresh and bright with new paint and a very pretty thing to see.

"Now," said Uncle Anson, "wait till you hear it strike!"

"Oh dear," said Aunt Gertrude. "Does it strike? Yes, I suppose it has to."

"But not like any other clock you ever heard!" warned Uncle Anson, his mild face beaming with pride. He wound it carefully and set the hands near twelve. They stood and listened as the clock began to tick toward the hour. Even Ada, with Sweetheart in her arms, came up to watch. Suddenly there was a whirring and a click. The egg in the nest opened like a door and out came a little bird. Jerkily it spread its wings, wings made of real red feathers tipped with black.

"Good heavens!" shrieked Aunt Gertrude, her hand flying to her heart. "It's a kneeknock bird! Anson! You dared to make a kneeknock bird!"

In Ada's arms, Sweetheart stiffened and the tip of his tail began to twitch.

"Listen!" cried Uncle Anson. "Listen!"

The wooden bird miraculously opened its beak and began to sing. "Awk-awk weep!" trilled the bird. "Brrrr weep-weep!"

A rust-colored blur shot from Ada's arms and in a tangle of fur and red feathers the clock bounced off its peg and fell to the floor. There was a crash, a confused metallic sound of liberated springs and spinning gears, a last protesting "Weep-weep!" and then silence. And in the middle of the smashed debris sat Sweetheart, his yellow eyes glowing, and in his jaws the broken wooden body of the little bird.

"But I don't understand," burst out Egan at supper. "Why didn't you *do* something to that cat? Chase him out of the house or *something!*" He looked over at the hearth, where Sweetheart sat contentedly washing his face.

Uncle Anson sighed heavily. He had been silent since the smashing of the clock and he was silent now.

"Well, why not tell him, Anson?" said Aunt Gertrude. "He ought to know these things if he's going to be visiting in Instep."

"I'll tell him, Mother," said Ada importantly. "Papa put a kneeknock bird into the clock, Egan. I guess he forgot about Sweetheart." (Uncle Anson made a strangled noise.) "Sweetheart thought it was real. Cats are supposed to kill kneeknock birds. The Megrimum wants them to."

Egan stared.

"Don't be such a big dumb, Egan," said Ada

with a superior frown. "Don't you know about kneeknock birds? They live in the trees at the top of the Rise. All the cats go up and kill them and bring them down. That's how Papa got the feathers, I suppose. The Megrimum likes cats. He keeps the kneeknock birds up there just for them. We can't go up to the top of the Rise, but the cats can. He likes them. And if people are mean to a cat, the Megrimum comes down and eats them up."

"What about dogs?" asked Egan, slipping a bit of meat to Annabelle where she sat under the table, her warm chin heavy on his knee.

"Dogs! Pooh!" said Ada scornfully. "Dogs are nothing special. They never climb up the Rise. Annabelle couldn't if she tried. She's too old and fat. No, cats are what the Megrimum likes. Just cats."

From the hearth came a low, self-satisfied rumble. Sweetheart was purring.

In the middle of the night Egan was jolted awake by a violent crash of thunder. In the sudden wind, raindrops pelted his window like handfuls of berries. Annabelle, who had been sleeping on the cot at his feet, lifted her head, listened, and began to tremble. With bulging eyes and tail pressed tight between her legs, she slid down and scrabbled under the cot, where she lay panting in the private darkness, bulky and pathetic with dread.

"Come on out, Annabelle," whispered Egan. "It's only rain." But she wouldn't budge. The rain increased and thunder boomed again. As the rumble ebbed, Egan heard a soft knock at his door and Ada, small and ghostly in a white nightdress, tiptoed into the room. Her red hair, unbraided for the night, was wild about her shoulders and her eyes were saucers of excitement.

"Now you're going to hear it! Any minute now, Egan. Isn't it thrilling?" She perched cross-legged on the end of the cot with her nightdress tucked primly under her toes, and cocked her head to listen.

Egan listened, too. "I don't hear anything but rain and wind," he whispered.

"It'll start soon," she answered. "But don't be scared. Papa left a candle at the window like always, and a wishbone on the hearth. And Mother hung the onions on the door hinge."

"What's all that for?" asked Egan. A flash of lightning glared for an instant and they sat tensely, waiting for the thunder. It came with a roar that seemed to split the sky in two. From under the bed the pace of the dog's panting quickened.

"I suppose that's Annabelle under there," whispered Ada. "She's a big coward. Now Sweetheart, he's out somewhere in the storm. He loves it."

Egan ignored the slur against his friend. "What're the candle and the wishbone for?" he asked again.

"My goodness, Egan," sighed Ada. "Don't

you know anything? If you leave a candle in your window, the Megrimum knows you're safe inside. When it sees the wishbone, it thinks all the food is eaten up and there's none left to steal. And when it smells the onions on the door hinge . . ."

Just then, from somewhere high up in the night, a thin, wailing sound came riding down the wind. "That's it!" hissed Ada. "Listen! There it is. First time in a month!" She hugged her knees and bounced with pleasure. Egan jumped out of bed and ran to the window, pressing his face against the cold glass. The wail dimmed and then began again, deepened to a moan, hollowed, wavered, and was lost in another crash of thunder.

At the window Egan clutched the sill and stared out at the wet, swirling darkness. Leaves and twigs, caught by the wind, hurried up, paused, and were swept away, and the rain chased in rivers down the glass. Once more, from far above, the low moan came faintly to his ears. It rose slowly, threading to a wail again, and held for a long, terrible moment. Egan stood speechless, and Ada, coming to his side, was quiet herself for once. At last the wail drooped, dwindled, died. They waited, staring out into the storm. Suddenly, as lightning lit the darkness for a bright, white instant, they both saw at the same moment a dim shape coming down the rocky side of Kneeknock Rise, just beyond the garden wall. They clutched each other. "Did you see that? What can it be? Hide! *Quick!*" They sprang to the cot, tearing at the quilts, and buried their heads. Thunder, farther off now, muttered briefly and then, through the thinning rain, they heard a tapping at the window. Egan's heart thumped like a drum as he huddled frozen on the cot. The dreadful tapping came again and then, quite suddenly, Annabelle stopped panting and began to bark. At the same moment, the bedroom door burst open and they heard Aunt Gertrude calling. "Egan! What's the matter?" Then, a shriek: "Oh, mercy! Anson! There—there at the window!" She screamed once, shrill as a whistle, and fainted into a heap. And Anna-belle, emerging from under the cot, stood with her front paws on the windowsill, barking on and on against the glass, which now showed nothing but the empty, drizzling dark.

$$\bowtie$$

By breakfast time the news of the family's ter-rible nighttime visitor had spread all over In-step, for Ada had hurried to tell a talkative neighbor or two, and any event to do with Kneeknock Rise, however mild or serious, was considered the rightful property of the entire village. The morning air was chilly after the rain, and Aunt Gertrude, limp on a bench at the hearth, beside a crackling fire, held court to a stream of eager visitors. To each she described the thunder and the moans from the top of the Rise (these they had all heard for themselves, but they listened anyway—it was her right, in view of what had happened, to speak for the entire night) and then, as they

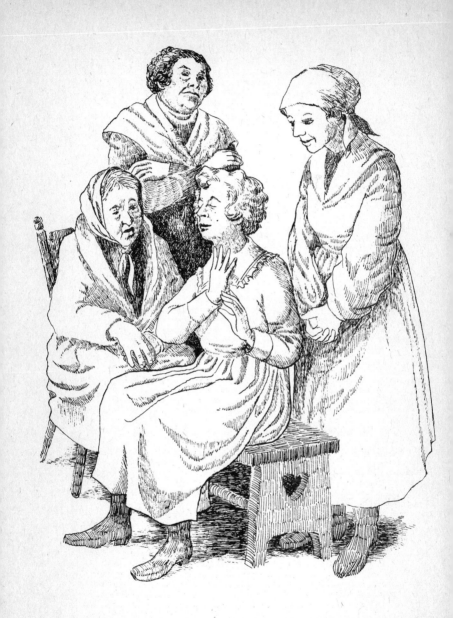

leaned breathlessly toward her, she tried, faintly but with emotion, to describe what she had seen at the window.

"A kind of a face, it was, but very white, with a wild glow around it. Two eyes, I think —though there may have been three. I don't recall a nose at all, but the mouth was just a big black hole. Oh, dreadful, dreadful! I can hardly bear to think about it." The visitors would cluck sympathetically and go away, some nervously, and some rather jealously. Egan heard one woman say to her friends as they left the house, "If Gertrude and Anson had only bought that weathervane I tried to sell them, it never would have happened. Everyone knows that an iron weathercock will crow at times like that and scare the danger away."

"Nonsense," said one of the others. "A weathervane's no good. You have to grow poppies in your dooryard. No demon can stand the sight of poppies."

"Poppies are all very well when they're

blooming," said a third. "But the very best thing of all is still a bell. The devil himself will run when you ring a bell. It doesn't even have to be a very large bell."

The same kind of discussion went on in the little house all morning. And when Uncle Anson came home from his shop at lunchtime, Aunt Gertrude began on it again.

"For years, Anson, for *years,* mind you, we've been careful. Every night the candle, the wishbone, the onions. And in spite of it all, this terrible thing happens!"

"See here now, Gertrude," said Uncle Anson. "The Megrimum, if it *was* the Megrimum, couldn't have seen the candle *or* the wishbone from that back window. And he couldn't have smelled the onions, either."

"But that's just it!" cried Aunt Gertrude. "That's the very thing that makes us out so foolish! Don't you see? It never occurred to me before, but for all these years we've been assuming that if trouble came, it would come politely round to the front of the house—wipe its feet, even—and then knock on the door. The miller's wife pointed it out, of course. In front of everyone. I've never been so embarrassed. And they were right to laugh at us."

Uncle Anson frowned. "See here, Gertrude," he said, "I don't believe for a minute that the Megrimum *did* come down. He's got his place up there and we have ours down here. I think it was just a stranger coming early to the Fair who thought it would be funny to scare somebody."

"Perhaps you're right, Anson. A stranger wanting to scare somebody! I'm sure I never heard of anything so mean. Yes, yes, you must be right. Well, Annabelle was some use after all, wasn't she, with her barking? That stranger won't come *here* again."

Aunt Gertrude sighed with relief and gave Annabelle a large plate of the pancakes she had fixed for lunch. The old dog beamed at the unexpected reward and lay about all afternoon licking her syrupy whiskers contentedly. Just before supper, Egan heard his aunt say to a late-coming villager, "Well, it may have been the Megrimum and it may not. We scared it away, though. It won't come back soon again, whatever it was. You may be sure of that!"

But later she said to Uncle Anson, "Just the same, I do believe that clock of yours with the feathers and all was bad luck, Anson. Let's have no more of those feathers in this house again. Ever!"

"Perhaps you're right," said Uncle Anson.

><

With nightfall coming on, they gathered close to one another before the fire. There was a special coziness in being together now, after all the uproar of the night before. Uncle Anson smoked his pipe and dreamed into the flames, devising new and daring clocks, while Sweetheart, curled into a furry wad in Ada's lap, looked the very picture of innocence, a picture which from time to time he spoiled by stretching out a long foreleg and arching the claws wickedly from a taut, spread paw. Annabelle dozed on the hearth, snoring softly, and Egan poked at the fire with a stick, so nearly asleep that he jumped when Aunt Gertrude spoke to him. She was sitting on the bench, sewing, and she held out for his inspection a curious pouch-shaped object of bright, soft cloth.

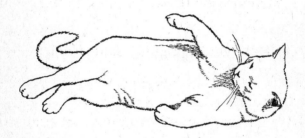

"There, Egan, what do you think of that?" she asked. "It's the last of forty sets."

Egan looked at the object doubtfully. "It's pretty, Aunt Gertrude. What is it?" he said.

Ada sighed. "You don't know *anything*, do you, Egan?" she accused.

"Why, it's to go over the legs of chairs or tables, dear. Couldn't you tell?" said Aunt Gertrude, peering anxiously at her handiwork. "To keep the floor from getting scratched. Four to a chair, and four to a table, too, of course. I've made them for years to sell at the Fair. Mar-no-mores, I call them. They sell very well, too. I'll send a set home with you for your mother." She tucked the bit of cloth into her sewing basket. "There! All finished. How about a story before bed, Anson?"

Uncle Anson yawned. "Not tonight, Gertrude. Too tired. Have to get to bed early. After all, tomorrow is the Fair. Lots to do at the shop."

Out on the road in front of the house someone in heavy boots came clumping along. Annabelle sat up, listened with lifted ears, and hurried to the door, her tail thrashing expectantly.

"No, Annabelle," said Uncle Anson gently. "That isn't Ott." The footsteps faded away down the road. Annabelle's tail drooped. She

40

turned away from the door and lay down again heavily, her brown eyes empty. "Poor old dog," murmured Uncle Anson.

"Why did Uncle Ott go away, anyhow?" asked Egan.

"Ott is never happy in one place for long," said Uncle Anson. "He's a funny fellow in some ways, and then in some ways he's remarkable. Only thing he likes is reading and verses. And travel. He'll be away for weeks and then he'll get one of those wheezing spells of his. Trouble with his breathing. So he comes back here and rests till he's better and then he wanders off again. He always took the dog along before, though. Don't know why he left her this time. It isn't like him, and that's what worries us."

"The Megrimum ate him," crooned Ada.

"Hush, Ada!" said her father roughly. "That's nonsense. Ott wouldn't have climbed the Rise. He has too much sense for that. No, he'll come back one of these days with all sorts of stories about where he's been. I just hope he doesn't stay away too long. Annabelle's getting on. She won't be able to travel about much longer."

"How old is she?" asked Egan.

"Annabelle? Oh, well, I guess she must be eleven or thereabouts. Twelve, maybe. That's a lot of years for a dog." Uncle Anson stood up and stretched. "Bedtime, everyone," he rumbled, and then he paused and turned shyly to Egan. "By the way, Nephew, would you like to see some of Ott's verses? They're not too bad, as a matter of fact." He took a small sheaf of papers from the mantelpiece and held them out. "They're really—well, that is, they're not too bad, even if he *is* my brother. Look them over."

"I'd like to," said Egan truthfully.

"Certainly. That's all right. Go right ahead," said Uncle Anson, as if the whole idea had been Egan's. He beamed at his nephew suddenly, gave him the papers, and marched off to bed.

Egan opened his bedroom window and leaned out. The dark bulk of Kneeknock Rise hunched against a sky rich in stars. There would be no storm tonight to disturb the sleep of the Megrimum. Egan leaned out farther, sniffing the chilly air, and craned his neck to see the top of the cliff. As always, it was hidden in its cuff of mist, mist made luminous now by the frosty stare of a newly risen moon. What would it be like, he wondered, if he himself were to climb to the top and slay the thing that dreamed there? He would come down again with its head on a stick and they would be so proud of him. He would be famous . . . A gust of wind fled by and from the clifftop came a restless sighing sound, faint and sad. Egan sighed himself, and drew in his head, closing the window softly. "The poor old thing seems harmless enough tonight," he said to Annabelle, who was stretched once again across the foot of the cot. He scratched behind her ears and she licked his fingers. Then he settled himself on the cot, his back against the wall, and lifted the first sheet from the little pile of verses. The writing was round and graceful and clear in the candlelight and Egan began to read:

What's on the other side of the hill?
    Hush, they told me. No one knows.
I'll climb and see for myself! I will!
    Thus I bravely, gravely chose.
Up I climbed, for I had to know.
    (Castles? Caverns? Oceans? Rills?)
Curiosity drew me so.
    (Kings in velvet and fools in frills?)
Nobody's going to make me stop.
    I'll climb, I said, and see. I will!
Here's what I saw when I reached the top:
    Another hill.

"Hmmmm," said Egan. He wasn't sure what the poem meant, but he liked the sound of it. He picked up the next sheet:

Tame as butter and wild as bears,
  Annabelle snores and no one cares.
Annabelle eats without a spoon.
  Nobody scolds if she sleeps till noon.
And Annabelle strolls in the marketplace
  With nothing on but her awkward grace.
But I wear hats and must live with hope,
  And polish my face with terrible soap
And hide my verses and show my smiles
  And listen to everyone else's trials.
Annabelle's lucky. Annabelle's free.
  And she chose to be slave to the likes of me!

This was better. Egan smiled and smoothed Annabelle's flank with his toes. "Uncle Ott loves you and so do I," he told her. She opened one bleary eye, hiccupped, and went back to sleep. "Oh well," he said indulgently, and picked up another verse:

I visited a certain king
  Who had a certain fool.

The king was gray with wisdom got
  From forty years of school.
The fool was pink with nonsense
  And could barely write his name
But he knew a lot of little songs
  And sang them just the same.
The fool was gay. The king was not.
  Now tell me if you can:
Which was perhaps the greater fool
  And which the wiser man?

Egan laid aside the verses. He blew out his
candle and climbed in under the quilts, dou-
bling his knees under his chin so as not to disturb Annabelle, who still occupied the foot of
the cot. He wound his arms around the pillow
and lay thinking about Uncle Ott. "I wish," he
said to himself, "that I could have seen him.
He must be very wise, like the king in the
poem. Or rather, like the fool. Except that I
think he must be gay and wise both at the same
time. Unless perhaps that's impossible." He

tried to decide about the king and the fool but
it was too immense a problem for so late at
night. And, anyway, he was very sleepy. All at
once he longed to stretch out his legs. His knees
twitched. It was intolerable to keep them dou-
bled up a moment longer. He tried Annabelle's
bulk with an anxious toe. Nothing happened.
He pressed both feet against her back through
the covers and she woke, growled once, and
made herself heavy as a boulder. "Get down,
Annabelle, for goodness' sake," he said, push-
ing hard. At last the old dog sighed dramatically.
She heaved up, reproached him with a hard
look in the dimness, and gave up her soft hollow
for the cold floor, where, for perhaps a minute,
she lay awash with self-pity. Then a snore.
Sleep had claimed her again.

Egan turned over onto his stomach and eased
his toes into the warmth the dog had left behind. Outside, the wind carried the faintest
hint of a lullaby, crooned wearily from the top
of Kneeknock Rise. The problem of the king and

the fool dissolved into muted patterns of velvet which rippled, wavered, and lifted him away into sleep.

✂

Egan had a most peculiar dream that night. He imagined that he was a king wrapped in a cloak made of velvet that strongly resembled Annabelle's ears. There was a fool with him who looked at him and laughed and said, "You're all dog-eared, Your Majesty," and Egan was angry at the fool for making fun of him; but when he looked closer, he saw that the fool was himself.

Then Aunt Gertrude was beside him, wielding a needle with thread like rope. "Don't worry, Your Majesty," she shrieked in his ear. "I'll sew the feathers on again if you'll just give me the time. Give me the time! Give me the time!"

He discovered that he was carrying a clock in his arms. He held it out to his aunt but it slipped out of his fingers and smashed, and dozens of little red birds fluttered out of the wreckage.

"Don't you know *anything*?" scolded the fool who was also himself.

"He went to school for forty years but he can't even write his name," jeered Aunt Gertrude.

The rope she carried suddenly became a long red pigtail. Aunt Gertrude had turned into Ada. "Don't go! Don't go!" cried Ada, dragging at his cloak.

But he was climbing now, climbing in the dark, up and up an endless hillside. Someone was with him and he knew without looking that it was his Uncle Ott.

"Do you think we ought to go?" he heard himself asking.

"Oh, yes! Indeed we ought. Ott. Ott!" said his uncle, and they both laughed.

Then they were at the top of the hill. It was sunny and the ground was covered with wishbones. "Now we can slay the Megrimum," he said, but his uncle pointed down.

"No, no, forget the Megrimum and look. See what's on the other side."

There was another hilltop almost at their feet and Sweetheart was sitting on it, waving his tail. He was wearing a set of Aunt Gertrude's Mar-no-mores over his paws.

"That's all right," said Egan. "Now he can't scratch."

All at once he was aware of a noise, a kind of roar-whistle roar-whistle, and he found himself waving a huge bouquet of poppies. The poppies were heavy as iron and he could only wave them very, very slowly. The roar-whistle noise grew louder and suddenly the person at his side turned into Ada.

"The Megrimum is coming," she cried. "You were a fool to climb the Rise."

Then he was running, but his feet were so heavy that he could hardly lift them and the noise was louder than ever.

"But it's only a bell," he heard himself say, and discovered at once that he could now run very swiftly. "Don't be afraid," he called as he skimmed down the hillside. "It's a bell and a bell an' a bell an' a bell . . ."

Suddenly he was wide awake and sitting up in his cot. On the floor beside him, Annabelle was snoring. Whistle-roar whistle-roar. He leaned over the edge of the cot and prodded her gently. The snoring stopped. He stretched out under his quilts and went back to sleep and did not dream again.

"You look tired," said his aunt at breakfast. "Didn't you sleep well?"

"I had a funny dream," said Egan, "and then Annabelle snored and woke me up."

"Nobody in Instep sleeps well," sighed Aunt

Gertrude. "We're all nervous. You're getting that way, too. It's living so near to the Rise that does it."

"Why doesn't everyone move away?" asked Egan.

Aunt Gertrude looked shocked. "What an idea!" she said. "Never mind. You'll stop feeling nervous when you go home."

"Home is going to seem kind of dull after Instep," sighed Egan.

Aunt Gertrude beamed and gave him another plate of eggs. "That's it exactly," she said.

≫≪

The Instep Fair! For months they planned and worked toward this one day and for months the people in the surrounding countryside looked forward to it eagerly. It was the crown of the calendar, the jewel of the year, and now, from miles around, the people were arriving. They came in carts, in caravans, on foot, all dressed in their holiday clothes and carrying baskets, boxes, and bundles packed with picnics so special and exotic that even the most finicky of the children were frantic for suppertime.

The village square was ringed by a crowd of little booths hung in rainbows of fluttering cloth, and by ten o'clock it was jammed with happy, milling people. At one corner a platform had been raised and a troupe of dancers whirled there to the thin, gay music of flutes and pipes. Everywhere tradesmen were inviting: "Hot sausage while it lasts!" "Beads here—bracelets! Buy for your sweetheart!" "This way! This way! Try your luck! Three hoops and you can't miss!" And all the shops in the village were brave with flags, bright new merchandise spilling out of their doors into the street on trays and tables and mats. Uncle Anson had set his clocks so that one or another was striking every minute and cuckoos of every description were popping in and out of their little doors like nosy neighbors. The color! The noise! And the smells— cider, and apples, and the perfume of great ropes of taffy folding and stretching in the buttery, knowing fingers of the candy-makers; the crisp, dry smell of stacks of woven wicker baskets; the sterile, fussy smell of just-completed quilts and rugs; and the best smell of all, the take-me-home smell, the smell of brand-new painted wooden toys. Happy confusion was everywhere. Dogs barked and children ran shouting after them and mothers ran after the children and the men stood about rumbling and smoking, grave with pleasure.

It was dazzling. Thrilling. And exactly like all fairs everywhere, large or small, except for one thing: everyone here was hoping for bad weather. When townspeople met on the street, they shook their heads and murmured to each other: "It looks bad! Not a cloud in sight." And the visitors interrupted their rounds continually to stare up at the dark silence of Kneeknock Rise. "What do you think? Will there be a storm?" "There'd better be." "But look at that sky! Blue as a lake." "They say it always sleeps

in good weather. Takes rain to wake it up."
"Well, I walked twenty miles to get here. I'm
going to stay until I hear it and that's that."

But shortly after twelve a single cloud, no
more than a wisp, appeared on the horizon.
When they spotted it, everybody cheered and
pointed and the townspeople, rosy with relief,
went round again more importantly than ever,
telling their tales of the Megrimum with fresh-
ened pride. The modest little cloud, all unaware
of the role it was playing, drifted slowly forward, and behind it, like a troop of watchful
nurses, a great piled hump of clouds rose up,
and another and another, till a whole regiment
came marching into the sky. In the square the
merrymaking grew noisier than ever. It was going to be a splendid day.

Into the center of it all, that afternoon, came
Egan, dazzled and breathless with the glories
of his first fair. He clutched in his pocket a

handful of coins saved for months toward this very moment and he beamed without knowing he was beaming. At his side, Ada, veteran of many fairs, did her best to appear bored and critical, pointing out this feature and that and comparing each to its predecessors of other years. But she was flushed with excitement and the pleasure of having a friend to whom she could show off the Fair, and very proud of her new blue dress and the blue ribbon on the end of her pigtail. Behind them strolled Annabelle, pointedly ignoring the coarse carouse of other dogs. She threaded primly through forests of legs, her nose quivering. The scents were delicious; she sniffed them expertly, sorted out that of a nearby sausage booth, and turned toward it hopefully. Years of experience had taught her that children were careless. They dropped things, often things to eat. The smell of the sausage glazed her eyes with greed. Yes, it was going to be a splendid day.

Egan walked with Ada once around the ring of booths, inspecting everything carefully. He was going to buy, but he refused to be hurried. He barely nodded to his father's friend, the chandler who had driven him to Instep, for he had no interest in anything so dull as candles. At last he stopped before a booth where beaded necklaces and bracelets spilled in gaudy heaps over a tangle of bright silk scarves and ribbons. He was charmed, caught. He stepped forward, clinking the coins in his pocket.

"What are you going to do?" said Ada. She was impatient to move on to an enchanting little proscenium of red and yellow stripes, where a puppet show was stirring a crowd of children to squeals of laughter.

"I'm going to buy a present," said Egan. "A present for my mother."

"That's right! What a dear, good lad!" cooed the woman who was tending the booth.

"Do you mean you're going to buy your mother a dumb old bracelet? Or one of those awful scarves?" asked Ada. "That's a waste of money."

The woman inside the booth scowled at Ada and turned to Egan persuasively, holding up a necklace of shiny red beads. "Look here, darling," she said. "Isn't that just bee-yoo-tiful? Your mother will love it. And here's a bracelet to match." She dropped the beads into his hand. They felt cool and made a most agreeable clicking sound.

"I'll buy them," he croaked, helpless but pleased, and then, on an impulse, "I'll buy that, too," and pointed to a square of blue silk that had a little cat painted carefully on one corner. He took it from the woman and handed it to Ada. "That's for you," he said brusquely.

"Well!" said Ada, mollified. "Thank you very much. It's just bee-yoo-tiful!" She tied the scarf around her neck at once, but as they left the booth she turned and made a face at the woman anyway, just for good measure.

They watched the puppet show twice through, drank brimming cups of cider, bought apples, and went around again, munching. There were games to play—toss the hoop over the peg; throw the beanbag through the hole; guess how many pebbles in the jar. For these games and all the others, there were shiny prizes which nobody ever won, which, in fact, nobody ever expected to win. The prizes were too grand, and the game operators too haughty, and the games themselves, after all, too difficult. How could you possibly be expected to toss the hoop over the peg when the game operator stared at you so, jingling the money in his apron pocket in that superior way? When the others waiting their turn were so impatient? And anyway, the hoop was very small and the peg was very far away. After each game there was a moment when you felt clumsy and resentful, but there was always another booth, another game, another lift of hope, and so it went round and round, all through the afternoon.

But buying presents was the best of all. Egan

chose a pipe for Uncle Anson, with *Instep Fair* painted around its bowl in curling letters. He bought a pretty packet of needles for Aunt Gertrude, and for his father, a large, polished wishbone pried, no doubt, from the roasted breast of some hapless goose. Fastened to the wishbone was a small card which advised: *It's best to be safe.*

"What do you want that for?" asked Ada. "There isn't any Megrimum where you live."

"That's all right," said Egan. "It's a souvenir."

"They shouldn't sell things like that just for souvenirs," frowned Ada. "They ought to take it more seriously."

"I don't see why," said Egan. "Come on, let's go sit down somewhere. My money's all gone and my legs are tired out."

⚹

And all the time the clouds were coming, those hoped-for guests of honor, crowding against each other till at last the sun was lost and the sky hung low and gray. The square had begun to empty now, for it was nearing suppertime. The visitors were strolling off to their carts and caravans, calling to each other of tents and campfires, and the villagers were closing up their shops. A breeze, bustling across the square, set the flags and banners to flapping and the sky darkened.

"It's going to be a big one!" cried somebody.

A group of visitors hurried past the patch of grass where Egan and Ada had dropped, and their faces were tense with excitement. It appeared that the feature of the day was about to begin and this, after all, was what they had really come for. A storm was on the way and they would hear the Megrimum. It would wake on its clifftop and they would hear it moan. "There! Listen! Wasn't that thunder?" "No, not yet. Come on! Let's find a place to wait out of the weather."

The sausage man was nailing boards across the open front of his booth on the other side of the square. Egan and Ada, immobilized by cider and fatigue, sat watching him as the rising wind belled his apron and bits of paper twirled across the grass. Then they heard him shout: "Get out of there, blast you! Come away from that meat!" He vanished behind his booth, waving his arms, and Annabelle appeared on the other side, chewing hurriedly.

"Annabelle!" called Egan. "Here, Annabelle!"

The old dog started across the square toward them and then she paused. A low rumble of thunder filled the sky and the clouds seemed to tremble. Annabelle broke into a run, her fat body bouncing over the grass. In a moment she reached them and crouched against Egan's side, her eyes glassy.

"That dog certainly is a sissy," said Ada crossly. The Fair was over and her new blue dress was dusty and wrinkled. She frowned at Egan, who sat sorting over the presents he had bought. "Let me see that old wishbone," she said, and snatched it from him.

"Annabelle is not a sissy," said Egan, frowning back. "What's the matter with you? She can't help it if she doesn't like storms. Anyway, we'd better go home. It's going to rain. Give me back that wishbone."

"It's not going to rain for hours yet," cried Ada, angry that the day was ending. "What's the matter with *you*? I'll bet you're afraid, too. Sissy! Sissy! Here's your stupid wishbone." She dropped it into his lap, sprang up, and began to dance around him. The wind tossed her skirt about her knees and her pigtail bounced. "Sissy sissy sissy!" she sang.

Egan's face grew hot. "I am not a sissy!" he shouted. Thunder rolled a little nearer and Annabelle pressed against his legs, panting.

Ada stopped dancing suddenly and bent over him. "If you're not a sissy, prove it," she said, her nose close to his.

"What do you mean?" asked Egan.

"You know," whispered Ada. "You know. Climb it, Egan. Climb up Kneeknock Rise!"

Egan stared at her.

"There! You see?" she cried. "You're afraid. Egan's afraid! Egan's afraid!" And she began to dance around him again.

Egan got slowly to his feet. Why not go? He wanted to. He had wanted to all along. He thought again of what it would mean to slay the Megrimum. To bring its head down on a stick! Excitement washed over him and he trembled.

"I'll show you!" he shouted. "I'll show you I'm not afraid, or Annabelle, either. We'll climb it together, both of us. You'll see!" And he turned toward the cliff.

Ada stopped her dance abruptly. Her face as she peered at him in the dim light was suddenly very pale. "No, Egan! I didn't mean it!" She tugged at his jacket. "Don't go! Don't go!"

But Egan pulled away, suddenly possessed by the dream he had had, lost in it, part of it. He was running away toward the cliff, fearless and wild, and the old dog ran after him.

"You're a big dumb fool!" screamed Ada into the wind. "The Megrimum will eat you just like it ate Uncle Ott!" She began to cry and then she was running, too, running away toward home just as the rain began.

❧❧

In the fields at the edge of the village, the visitors to the Instep Fair sat eating their suppers in a state of high excitement and anticipation. The rain fell softly at first, hissing into campfires and pattering gently on the sloping canvas of tents and the thin board roofs of caravans. Eager voices babbled, called, whispered.

"Ooh, I'm scared to death! When will it begin?" This happily.

"There's a lot more to the world than meets the eye. There's hidden things, strange things. That old fellow up there in the mist—it makes you stop and wonder. He can do terrible things. Great things, maybe. Who knows?" This soberly.

"I tell you there's nothing like it anywhere else in the world. I've traveled and I know." This proudly.

"Sheep and bread and the flat fields, that's what the days are. Except for this day. But it's enough, just having this day. It's the knowing there's something different, something special up there waiting. It's the knowing you could choose to change your days—climb up there and throw yourself right down the throat of the only and last and greatest terrible secret in the world. Except you don't climb up. A secret like that—well, it's worth the keeping. And anyway, you'd never come down again, ever." This with intense satisfaction.

The rain began to fall a little harder now. And all the while Egan was climbing up Kneeknock Rise, and Annabelle climbed after him.

"Stop crying, Ada! Calm yourself!" said Uncle Anson harshly. "I can't understand a thing you're saying!"

Aunt Gertrude stood rigid as a post, her hand on her heart, staring at her daughter.

"It's Egan, Papa! Egan," sobbed Ada. "He did it! I teased him, Papa, and he did it. He wouldn't stop."

"*What* did he do, Ada? What did Egan *do?*" cried Uncle Anson, gripping her shoulders firmly.

"Oh, Papa," she gulped, turning her face away from the alarm in her father's eyes. "It's all my fault. I dared him and he's doing it now. He's climbing, Papa. Climbing Kneeknock Rise."

"Merciful heavens!" gasped Uncle Anson, and behind him Aunt Gertrude sagged and dropped in a faint to the floor.

≫≪

And all the while Egan was climbing. Up and up over rocks and weeds, up between the twisted trees, panting with excitement. From time to time he paused, waiting for Annabelle to catch up with him. The dog's sides were heaving and her tongue dangled sidewise from her jaws, but her stiff old legs churned steadily along and her eyes were bright. Then all at once it began to rain in earnest, blurring the dim light and shellacking the rocks into slippery, treacherous jewels. Egan leaned against a tree trunk to catch his breath and Annabelle dropped down at his feet. He bent over to scratch her ears and then, suddenly, the moaning began.

It was loud here, halfway up the Rise, loud and horrifying and desperate. Down through the trees it twisted with the wind, a long, unearthly moaning that rose gradually till it wound into a high and hollow wail. Egan stood transfixed with his hand on Annabelle's head and for the first time he was afraid.

The Megrimum was awake at last. In the fields below, the chattering ceased. Faces peered out of tent flaps and windows, serious, frightened, eager. Here and there a man or a child came out into the rain and stood quietly, listening. An old woman dragged a stool from under a little cart and sat clutching an onion, nodding with her eyes tight shut, while the rain wilted her bonnet down around her ears.

But in the village there was frantic activity. Uncle Anson, a lantern bobbing from his hand, was rushing from neighbor to neighbor. "Quick! Quick! To my house at once! Yes, it's my nephew, my wife's sister's child. He's trying to climb the Rise. We've got to stop him. What do you mean, I'm crazy? We can't just let him go!"

Soon a wet and anxious group of men were arguing and shouting before the fire in the little house, while Ada snuffled miserably in a corner and Aunt Gertrude rushed back and forth, making coffee and spilling more than she served.

"But see here, Anson, that boy won't climb all the way up!" said one of the men.

"How do you know he won't?" answered Uncle Anson grimly. "He doesn't live in Instep. He doesn't understand."

"But good lord, man," cried another, "do you realize what you're saying? You're asking us to climb the Rise!"

"I know what I'm asking!" shouted Uncle Anson. "How can you think I don't? But can I let that boy stay out there now? The Megrimum is wide awake. I've never heard it moan so loud."

"Nobody would be fool enough to climb up there," growled another man.

"That boy is fool enough, bless him," said

Uncle Anson. "And I know my brother Ott would have climbed in an instant to save him. There's fools and fools, my friend. I'm going. Gertrude, where's my cap? I'm going and I'll go alone if I have to."

"I'll go, then," said one man.

"I, too," said another. "And I'll bring along my bell." And then they were all going, hurrying out into the drenching rain while high above the moaning rose and fell, winding and rippling like ribbon down the night.

⋙⋘

But Egan was half an hour ahead by that time. And he was young and strong, alone—and determined. After his first fear, he had clenched his fists and scowled. His early jealousy of the cliff's high pride returned. He searched about him among the trees and found a long, sharp stick.

"Look out up there!" he yelled into the rain. "I'm coming up!"

Off he went again, Annabelle struggling along

behind him. And by the time his rescuers were beginning the climb, Egan had come nearly to the top, and the mist that hung there reached out gently and gathered him in.

✄

Egan stood uncertainly in the mist. The rain was easing off. There had been no sound from the Megrimum for many minutes now. A mumble of thunder complained from far away and then the clouds parted and the moon rode free. Instantly the mist was luminous, and Egan, with a gasp, felt as if he had suddenly been tucked inside a bubble. Looking up, he saw the moon as a shapeless radiance, like a candle seen through steamy glass. Each drop of moisture in the mist had become a tiny prism, filtering and fanning the dim light into a million pale rainbows of softest color. From a shrouded treetop nearby came the soft, clear notes of a bird's call and, with the faintest of rustles, a small red kneeknock bird floated through the mist ahead of him. Egan held his breath and stared at the magic world around him, a night-time world bewitched into seeming morning by the wizard moon. Annabelle stood silent at his feet, and then, all at once, the old dog stiffened and whined. Nudged in his trance, Egan bent to soothe her but she pulled away from his hand, her ears high. She whined again, moved forward, stopped with tilted head, listening. Then with a yelp she ran on into the mist and disappeared. From somewhere up ahead a low groan echoed and Egan, his stick in his hand, moved slowly after Annabelle, straight toward the very top of Kneeknock Rise.

❧

On the cliffside below, the rescuers paused.

"The storm is over. Look, there's the moon!" said one of the men. "And the Megrimum's been quiet for quite a while now."

"Look here, Anson," said another. "I think we should search around a bit. That boy of yours can't have gone all the way up. He must be somewhere about."

"Perhaps," said Uncle Anson. "We'll divide up and look. But if we don't find him, I'm going on to the top."

With swaying arcs of lantern light washing the dark, the men spread out among the trees along the side of the Rise. Below, in her garden behind the little house, Aunt Gertrude stood wringing her hands. She could hear, faintly, the tinkling of the bell, warning away the Megrimum, and heard as well the distant, muffled voice of her husband calling: "Egan! Egan! Where are you, Nephew? E-e-e-gan!"

Out in the fields, the visitors knew something had happened.

"A boy, you say?"

"What? Climbing up the Rise?"

"A terrible thing—terrible. It called the child, perhaps, called the child to climb."

"Where was the boy's mother, then, to let him run away?"

"They're climbing up to find him. Look—see the lights of the lanterns."

"Brave men, brave men all."

"Never come down again, ever."

❧

Egan, deep in the mist, heard nothing. He wandered up the final stony slope toward the top like a sleepwalker lost in dreams. The heavy air around him, tinted and dim and moist, was growing unaccountably warmer, and a faint, unpleasant smell he could not quite recognize crept into his nostrils. And then he stopped, chilled suddenly out of his trance. Just ahead there came a noise as of an animal thrashing about, and the low rumble of a voice.

He crept forward, grasping the nearly forgotten stick tightly, and his heart pounded. The Megrimum! At last, the Megrimum! Slay it, perhaps—perhaps; but at least he would see it.

More thrashing in the weeds ahead. "Owanna-ooowanna," the voice seemed to murmur.

Closer and closer crept Egan and then he saw it dimly, all flailing arms, rolling about on the ground.

Another few cautious steps, and then:

"Oh, Anna, Anna, dear old dog!" crooned the voice. There before him, sitting on the ground, was a wild-haired, laughing man who had to be his Uncle Ott, engulfed and struggling happily in the wriggling, wagging ecstasy of Annabelle.

Egan stood with his mouth hanging open. The stick dropped from his hand, and at the sound the man and the dog paused in their greeting and looked toward him. Annabelle trotted over and beamed at him and then turned back.

"Hallo there, boy. Who might you be?" said the man warily.

Egan gulped. "Why, I'm your nephew. Sort of. That is, if you really *are* my Uncle Anson's brother. Are you? Are you Uncle Ott?"

"That's right!" said Uncle Ott in great surprise. "And you—you must be Anson's wife's

sister's boy. I guess I've got that right. But what in the name of goodness are you doing up here?"

"I came . . ." Egan paused. "Well, I came to kill the Megrimum." He waited for his uncle to laugh or scold, but Ott did neither. He merely nodded as if it were all quite natural. "But where *is* the Megrimum?" asked Egan. "And why is it so awfully warm up here?"

Uncle Ott stood up and brushed bits of twigs and leaves from his clothes.

"The Megrimum. Yes. I came to find it, too." He paused and looked thoughtfully at Egan and then, in a rush, he said, "Boy, listen to me. There isn't any Megrimum. Never was. It's all been just a lot of nothing all these years. Just a lot of—megrimummery, if you will. It's too bad, that's what it is. Too bad. Come along. I'll show you."

Close to the top of Kneeknock Rise lay a shallow cave. At the mouth of the cave the mist was very thick and as hot as steam, and the strange, unpleasant smell was almost overwhelming.

"Phew!" said Egan. "What in the world is in there? It must be something very rotten and dreadful!"

"No, not at all," said Uncle Ott. "It's only a mineral spring. Sulphur. Nasty, but not unnatural."

"A spring?" puzzled Egan. "But how could it be a spring? Springs aren't hot."

"Sometimes they are," said Uncle Ott. "This cliff must have been a volcano long ago. The water boils up to the top through a narrow hole, from far under the earth where it's very hot. And that makes this steamy mist. Usually the hole lets the steam through quietly, but when rain seeps into the hot places—more pressure, more steam. And the steam makes the whistling, whining, moaning sound as it shoots out the top of the hole. Just like a boiling kettle. The cave echoes and makes the sound even louder, and that, my dear boy, is the long-feared, long-loved Megrimum."

Egan stood and stared and then all at once he was very pleased. "I knew this old cliff wasn't so wonderful," he said. "Can I go in there and look at the spring?"

Uncle Ott shook his head. "Too hot," he said. "And anyway, there's not much to it. Just a hole in the ground and a lot of hot rocks." He shook his head again and sighed. "Too bad about that. Just a hole in the ground."

They turned away from the cave and walked back to where Annabelle sat waiting for them. "Come down to Instep with me and we'll tell them about it," said Egan. "We can both sleep in your room. I'll sleep on the floor with Annabelle."

"No, no, I think I won't go down to Instep," said Uncle Ott, running his fingers through his wild white hair. "Now that I've got my own dear Annabelle with me—and I do thank you for bringing her up—I guess I'll just go on down the other side."

"Have you been up here all the time?" asked Egan.

"Yes, as a matter of fact I have. I came up thinking I'd be going right back down again, so I didn't bring Annabelle along, and anyway, I was afraid she'd have trouble with the climbing. But when I got up here, the air was so wet and hot—well, it just did wonders for my wheezing. Absolute wonders. See? I can breathe perfectly well!" He took several deep breaths to show that it was true. "It's been a blessing. But now I guess I'll move along."

Egan had a sudden idea. "It was you that night, wasn't it? Tapping at the window?"

Uncle Ott looked embarrassed. "That was too bad. I thought I could get Annabelle to come to the window and then I could lift her out and take her away with me. But there was Gertrude all of a sudden, screaming, and I had to go away. I felt very bad about scaring her."

"But I don't see why you didn't just come into the house," said Egan. "During the day. And take Annabelle then."

"Because," said Uncle Ott slowly, "I didn't want to have to explain."

Egan was puzzled. "About the Megrimum, you mean?" he asked. "Why not? They're all scared to death of the Megrimum. They'd be happy to hear there isn't one after all."

"Do you think so?" said Uncle Ott. "I really don't know about that. I've been thinking and thinking about that." He looked at Egan sadly. "Is it better to be wise if it makes you solemn and practical, or is it better to be foolish so you can go on enjoying yourself?"

"The king and the fool!" said Egan, suddenly understanding.

"Exactly," said Uncle Ott. "Exactly. I see you've been reading my verses. I've been interested for years in this problem of kings and fools. Now here I am with a perfect example of the question and I really don't know the an-

swer." He sat down on the ground beside Annabelle and stared off into the mist, rubbing his
chin. "For me it's always been important to
find out the why of things. To try to be wise.
But I can't say it's ever made me happier. As
for those people down below, they've had their
Megrimum for years and years. And I don't
know as I want to spoil it all for them. There's
always the possibility that they're happier be-
lieving. Kind of a nice idea, this Megrimum."
He stood up and pulled his jacket close around
his chest, breathing the mist deeply. "Yes, it's
kind of a nice idea in an odd kind of way," he
said. "Do as you like about it. If I knew what

was best, I'd certainly tell you, but the fact is I don't. Well, come along, Annabelle. Goodbye, Nephew. A pleasure to have seen you."

He started off and then he paused and stood thinking for a moment. At last he turned and came back. "I've just had another thought on the matter," he said. "It came to me in rhyme. Thoughts often come to me that way—I don't seem to be able to help it:

> The cat attacked a bit of string
>   And dragged it by the head
> And tortured it beside the stove
>   And left it there for dead.
>
> "Excuse me, sir," I murmured when
>   He passed me in the hall,
> "But that was only string you had
>   And not a mouse at all!"
>
> He didn't even thank me when
>   I told him he was wrong.
> It's possible—just possible—
>   He knew it all along.

"Well, there it is, for what it's worth. Good-bye." Uncle Ott smiled and then, with Anna-belle wagging at his side, he turned and van-ished into the mist.

✄

When his uncle was gone, Egan went back again to the mouth of the cave and stood near the hot steam, listening to the gurgle of the spring and thinking. Then at last he said to himself, "Uncle Ott is pretty foolish after all. They don't know about this cave. They couldn't know and act the way they do. They'll be glad when I tell them the truth." He smiled. "I *did* slay the Megrimum, in a way. Or at least I'll slay it now." He picked up a good-sized rock that lay at the entrance to the cave and heaved it into the mist inside. There was a hollow, heavy *clink* and at once the gurgling stopped. Egan listened and then he grinned with elated sur-prise. "That's a pretty good shot," he crowed to himself. "That old rock will stop up the hole and there'll be no more moaning from *this* Megrimum!"

He realized all at once that he was wet to the skin and very hungry. He turned away from the cave and ran through the mist, emerging from its fringes into a cold, clear night. The moon was high and bright and below him the windows of Instep glowed snugly within the winking arc of the visitors' campfires. He stood looking down, clutching himself with pleasure over the news he was bringing, the great and staggering news. "I'll be famous," he whispered breathlessly. "They'll tell about what I did for years to come." A twinge of qualifying honesty nudged him and he added, "Of course, Uncle Ott will be famous, too. He came up first. And Annabelle!" He shivered and remembered again that he was wet and hungry. "Egan and Ott and *Ann*-a-belle," he sang under his breath as he bounded down the side of the Rise toward Instep. "Egan and Ott and *Ann*-a-belle; Anna-belle, Egan, and—OOF!" For he had bumped unseeing right into the arms of Uncle Anson.

"Egan! Egan, are you all right? Thank goodness I found you. Nephew—you didn't go all the way to the top, did you? Where's the dog?"

"Uncle Anson! Listen, Uncle Anson, listen! I *did* go all the way to the top! And guess who I found! Your brother was up there. Uncle Ott. And listen, Uncle Anson—I went and looked. There's nothing but a spring up there! A spring in a cave! There isn't any Megrimum aft—"

But Uncle Anson had clapped his hand over Egan's mouth. "Hush!" he cried. "Hush now. You're all excited. Probably coming down with a fever. Look, you're soaked through. Not another word. Not a peep. I'll have to get you home right away." He wrapped one arm firmly around Egan's shoulder and they started down the slope. Just below them in a clump of trees the lights of other lanterns glowed. "Hello! Hello down there!" called Uncle Anson, hustling Egan along. "I found him. He's all right. Let's go home."

But the rescuers were suddenly crowding around them, holding their lanterns high and peering with relief into Egan's face. "So you're safe! Foolish boy—you might have been killed. And think what we risked climbing up to save you!"

"But listen!" cried Egan, twitching out of Uncle Anson's grasp. "Listen! I went clear up there and looked and there isn't any Megri—"

"Where's the dog?" interrupted one of the men. "Anson, didn't you say he climbed with your brother's dog? That's a shame! The Megrimum got the dog, eh?"

"But there isn't any Me—" Egan began again.

"That boy looks feverish to me, Anson," said another man. "Better get him home right away. Too bad about the dog, but you're lucky the boy got away."

Egan began to shout. "Listen to *me!* I went and *looked.* There *isn't any Megrimum up there!*"

At once there was total silence. The men stood looking at him, expressionless. He looked back at them and felt a nudge of uncertainty. He said, more quietly, "There never *was* any Megrimum." The men waited, watching him. "It's only a spring in a cave," he finished in a very small voice.

After a long moment, one of the men cleared his throat. "No Megrimum. Well, that's certainly something. A spring in a cave. Hundreds of years—and no Megrimum." There was another uncomfortable silence and then they all started talking at once.

"Anson, that boy is feverish."

"Feverish? He's *delirious!* Better take him home."

"He doesn't know what he's saying."

"That's right—he doesn't know what he's saying."

And they turned away and started down the hillside, muttering to themselves.

Uncle Anson sighed and took Egan's hand. "Let's go home, Nephew."

"But look, Uncle Anson," Egan pleaded.

"There really isn't any Megrimum. Uncle Ott explained it all, all about the spring and the cave and everything. It's really true!"

Uncle Anson shrugged. "Perhaps. We'll talk about it later. Let's go home. It's been a long day."

❧❦

Egan sat on the bench before a blazing fire and sipped at a cup of scalding soup. He was draped with quilts and his feet tingled in a pan of steaming water. He wiggled his toes and sighed, and Uncle Anson, from his chair across the hearth, sighed too. On the floor between them Ada sat hugging her knees, nearly bursting with the questions she had been sternly ordered to keep to herself. Aunt Gertrude, on the bench beside Egan, stretched out cold fingers nervously to the flames. It was very quiet.

Finally Uncle Anson shifted in his chair and spoke. "Are you warmer now, Nephew? Feeling better?"

"Yes, thank you," said Egan. "But I felt all right before, too. I don't have any fever."

"I'm glad to hear it," said Uncle Anson.

And then Egan could contain himself no longer. "I saw what I saw," he said stubbornly, as if they had all been arguing, "and I don't see why you won't believe me."

Ada, too, erupted. "Tell us what you saw, Egan! Quick! Tell us all about it!"

"Well . . ." Egan looked toward Uncle Anson.

"All right. Go ahead and tell your story. We might as well have it now."

"Well!" said Egan again. "I climbed up the Rise and when I got to the mist at the top, Annabelle ran on ahead and I thought she'd found the Megrimum, but when I caught up with her, there was Uncle Ott!"

"Ott?" cried Aunt Gertrude. "Ott at the top of the Rise? And he was safe?"

"Where was the Megrimum?" Ada prodded.

"Uncle Ott was up there all the time," said Egan. He saw it again in his mind's eye—the tinted mist, the ghostly trees, and he warmed to his story. "It's all steamy up there. Uncle Ott said it made his breathing easier."

"Where was the Megrimum?" asked Ada again, clutching at his quilts.

"Uncle Ott showed me a cave at the top of the Rise," said Egan. He paused. This was the moment he had been looking forward to. "You should have been there, Ada. Guess what was in the cave!"

"The Megrimum!" cried Ada. "All hairy, with wings and lots of teeth!"

"Wrong!" declared Egan, looking around grandly. Aunt Gertrude was staring at him, quite speechless, her hand to her heart, but Uncle Anson sat with his eyes half closed, studying the fire. "Wrong," said Egan again, deciding to ignore his uncle. "There was a hole in the ground inside the cave. And a spring." And he went on to explain the secret as Uncle Ott had explained it to him. "And then," he finished, "he took Annabelle and he went away down the other side of the Rise."

When his story was over, there was a long

minute of silence. He sat waiting to be called a hero, or a savior, but no one spoke. At last Ada said, "Did you go into the cave to see what was there?"

"No," said Egan. "It was too hot. But I threw a rock in."

"You shouldn't have done that," said Aunt Gertrude. "He'll be angry because of that."

"But there's nothing up there to *get* angry," said Egan. "Don't you understand?"

"You didn't go inside the cave, though," said Ada. "You didn't really see."

"No," Egan began, "but . . ."

"He didn't want you to see him!" cried Ada triumphantly. "He hid in the cave in the mist!"

"That's it of course," exclaimed Aunt Gertrude with obvious relief. "How clever of you, Ada! And of course he hid from Ott, too. Don't you think so, Anson?"

"Perhaps," said Uncle Anson.

Egan was very annoyed. "Look here," he said loudly. "I went up there and nothing happened

to me. Uncle Ott was up there for *days* and nothing happened to him, either. And nothing happened to Annabelle."

"Maybe not," said Ada, "but it *could* have. Maybe he didn't feel like eating anybody just then. Maybe he wasn't hungry. Maybe you were too skinny. And Uncle Ott and Annabelle were too old and tough." She giggled.

"That's enough, Ada," said Uncle Anson. "Come along; it's bedtime. We'll get nowhere arguing like this. The whole thing can't be proved one way or another, anyway."

"Yes it can!" cried Egan. "It can be proved!"

"How?" asked Uncle Anson, frowning at him.

"I threw a rock right over that hole in the cave," said Egan. "Right over it. Wait till it rains again. There won't be a sound from up there. You'll see."

Ada got up from the hearth and opened the door. She peered up at the sky. "The moon's gone in," she announced. "There's a lot of clouds. Maybe it'll rain again tonight. I hope it does.

And then _you'll_ see, Egan. Won't he, Papa?"

"Perhaps, perhaps," said Uncle Anson wearily. "Come along to bed."

"Do you want to know something funny, Uncle Anson?" said Egan, frustration souring his manners. "You're always saying 'perhaps.' But Uncle Ott is different. _He's_ always saying 'exactly.'"

Uncle Anson looked at Egan sadly. "There are a lot of things Ott doesn't understand," he said.

"Uncle Ott understands _everything_," said Egan. "He's a very wise man."

"That's true," said Uncle Anson. "He _is_ a very wise man. But . . ."

"But," Aunt Gertrude interrupted, "he was a fool to climb the Rise. There's no perhaps about that. Go to bed, Egan. Ada. We'll talk again at breakfast."

It seemed to Egan that he hadn't closed his eyes all night. When, toward morning, the rain began to fall again, he lay waiting for Annabelle's nervous panting. Then he remembered. Annabelle was gone, gone with Uncle Ott down the other side of the Rise. Egan climbed out of bed and went to Ada's room. "Wake up!" he hissed at the warm lump under the quilts. "It's raining."

Ada sat up. "I heard it first," she said. "I was just coming in to wake *you* up."

"You were not, but never mind," said Egan. "Come on. We're going into my room and wait. I'm going to prove to you I'm right."

The rain came down gently and steadily. Egan opened his window and he and Ada leaned on the sill, staring out at the slope of Kneeknock Rise through the gray, wet glow of dawn.

"All right, then, where's the Megrimum?" asked Egan after a while. "I don't hear a thing." He grinned at Ada.

"You'll see, smarty," said Ada, not looking at him. "Be quiet. I'm trying to listen."

Something moved in the yard outside the window. "Look!" whispered Ada. "There's Sweetheart!" The cat emerged from the dim, dripping shrubbery and stood poised in the rain.

Then he sprang effortlessly to the top of the garden wall and disappeared over it. After a moment they caught another glimpse of wet orange fur starting up the side of the Rise. Ada pointed. "There he goes. He's climbing."

"Well," said Egan, "he won't find anything at the top."

"You'll see, smarty," said Ada again. "For goodness' sake, keep quiet."

After another long wait they heard footsteps behind them and Uncle Anson came into the room in his white nightshirt, his thin hair rumpled from sleep.

"What are you doing out of bed so early?" he asked, coming over to the window.

"It's raining, Papa," Ada explained.

"Yes," said Uncle Anson quietly, "I know."

"It's been raining for a long time," said Egan, "and there's not a sound from the top of the Rise!"

"Make him be quiet, Papa," begged Ada, close to tears at last. "The Megrimum's got to be up there! He's always been up there, Papa, hasn't he? He wouldn't go away."

"I think," said Uncle Anson, "we should all go back to bed."

Egan smiled to himself and was just turning away from the window when from high on the top of Kneeknock Rise came the muffled boom of an explosion, immediately followed by a high-pitched whistling shriek.

"It's the Megrimum!" cried Ada. "It's the Megrimum! You were wrong, Egan! He was up there all along! Listen, Papa."

The shriek cut thinly through the drizzling dimness, holding for a long moment. At last it broadened and dropped to the old, familiar moan. As they stood at the window staring out, a splash of orange fur came streaking into view down the side of the Rise, vaulted the garden wall, and paused for an instant in the yard.

"Sweetheart!" cried Ada.

The cat turned round, wild eyes to the faces peering out at him, and a second later hurled himself through the open window past them and was under the cot before Ada could make a move to catch him.

"What in the world was that?" cried Aunt Gertrude, appearing in the doorway.

"Something exploded on top of the Rise," said Uncle Anson.

"But it was only the rock," said Egan uncertainly. "It couldn't be the Megrimum because I went up there and I looked and Uncle Ott told me . . .''

"It's no use your arguing, Nephew," said Uncle Anson. "It's raining and the moaning has started and that's really all there is to it."

"Well, Sweetheart certainly is a sissy, anyway," said Egan loudly, looking sidewise at Ada. "He was so scared he came right in through the window."

But Ada only smiled. "I really like that scarf you bought for me, Egan," she told him. And then she turned to her mother and said: "Let's make a great big breakfast. There's no sense going back to bed now. Let's make a special breakfast to celebrate. Because of the Megrimum. He was up there all along."

❧❦

In the middle of the morning, Egan said goodbye to Ada and Aunt Gertrude and went slowly into the village and across the square into Uncle Anson's clock shop, where the chandler had promised to pick him up for the long ride home. The rain was still falling softly and the moaning from the top of the Rise could still be heard, though it had grown much fainter now and was sadder than ever. Egan leaned on the counter in the shop, his chin in his hand, and watched while his uncle wound up all the clocks for another day's ticking.

"Uncle Anson," he said at last, "was Uncle Ott right or wrong about the Megrimum?"

"I'm sure he thought he was right," said Uncle Anson. "I haven't climbed up myself, so I really can't say. I don't know what the real facts are."

"I can tell you one real fact," said Egan. "I certainly didn't see any Megrimum when I went up."

A cart creaked by in the street outside the shop and a passing villager called to the driver. "Headed home?"

"That's right. Back again next year. But I don't see how there could ever be another Fair as fine as this one was."

"Yes, it was just about perfect this year."

"Did that boy get down again safely?"

"Yes, I understand he was perfectly all right."

"I was sure of it. That old fellow up there would never harm a child. Well, see you next year."

"That's right. See you next year."

Egan glanced at his uncle but Anson was tinkering with the open works of a clock and didn't seem to have heard.

"Uncle Anson," said Egan.

"Ummmm," said Anson, looking up at last.

"Uncle Anson, please—tell me what you really think. Is there a Megrimum up there or isn't there?"

"Nephew," said Uncle Anson kindly, "I'll tell you what I think. I think it doesn't really matter. The only thing that matters is whether you want to believe he's there or not. And if your mind is made up, all the facts in the world won't make the slightest difference."

Egan was silent for a moment and then he

said, "But do you believe in the Megrimum?"

Uncle Anson laid aside the open clock. He stared out the shop window and rubbed his chin, just as Egan had seen Uncle Ott do at the top of the Rise. And then his expression changed to one of relief. "Look, Nephew, here comes the chandler. We'll have to finish our talk another year. Are you ready? It's time to go."

Suddenly Egan remembered. "My presents! I forgot about my presents! I left them in the square."

"Go see if you can find them, then," said Uncle Anson. "The chandler will wait."

Egan ran out of the shop and into the square, where a few men of the village were clearing away the last booths and flags. He hurried over to the spot where all of yesterday's adventures had begun. There on the grass lay the red beads he had bought for his mother and the pipe with *Instep Fair* still bright around its bowl. The packet of needles was there, too, though its gay cloth cover was soaking wet. But the wishbone was gone. Egan searched about in the grass and before long he found it. It was broken, splintered into sharp little fragments, and the card to which it had been fastened was wilted and smeared. Only the words *It's best* were still legible.

Egan sighed and, turning away, gathered up the other presents and hurried back to the clock shop. The chandler's cart was standing in the street and Frieda, the mule, appeared to be asleep, her harness drooping. Inside the shop the chandler and Uncle Anson were chatting.

"Here comes the boy," said Uncle Anson, looking up as Egan appeared in the doorway.

"Well, Egan!" said the chandler. "How did you enjoy the Instep Fair?"

"It was fine," said Egan, "but the present I bought for my father got broken somehow. Here, Uncle Anson, this pipe is for you, and would you give these needles to Aunt Gertrude for me?"

"Why, that's very kind of you, Nephew," said Uncle Anson. "But look here—why don't you take the pipe home and give it to your father? It would be a shame not to have a present for him."

"But then there's no present for *you*," Egan protested. "I wanted to do something for you."

"You've done something for me already," said Uncle Anson, smiling.

"I have?" wondered Egan. "What did I do?"

"You found my brother Ott. Remember? And you took Annabelle back to him. Now I won't be worried about either of them again."

"It sounds to me as if you've had a busy visit, Egan," said the chandler. "But no busier than that boy who tried to climb up Kneeknock Rise. You heard about that, I suppose?"

"Yes," said Uncle Anson. "We heard."

"He got down again all right, I understand," the chandler went on. "But they say he lost his dog to the Megrimum."

"Is that what they're saying?" asked Egan.

"I heard the whole story just now in the square," said the chandler. "Well, come along, Egan. Your mother will be anxious to have you home. Oh, by the way, would you like to have one of these souvenirs? I have an extra." He reached into his pocket and laid a polished wishbone on the counter. It was exactly like the one that lay in pieces in the square.

Egan picked it up and turned it over in his hands. "Thank you," he said, and then, echoing Ada: "But there isn't any Megrimum where we live."

"Better take it, just the same," said Uncle Anson, smiling at Egan. "Goodbye. Come back again next year."

"All right now, Frieda," said the chandler in a voice warm with encouragement. "Let's get a move on." The mule shook herself protestingly and clopped off down the street and around the square. Soon they had passed through the gates of Instep and were on their way across the level plains toward home.

Egan, sprawling in the empty straw behind the chandler, watched the village grow smaller and smaller. The rain had stopped and a feeble, watery sunshine filtered down through the clouds and touched the misty top of Kneeknock Rise with gold. The chandler looked back over his shoulder from the narrow seat and nodded at the cliff. "That's right," he said. "Give the old fellow some good weather and let him rest. He put on a splendid show for the Fair and now he must be tired."

"What if that boy, the one who climbed the Rise—what if he went all the way to the top and there wasn't anything there?" asked Egan.

"Well, I'll tell you something," said the chandler in a confidential tone. "In spite of what they say, I think it's more than likely lots of people have climbed up to look. And I'd be willing to bet that none of them saw a thing at the top. But he's up there just the same. What would you expect? That he'd come right out and shake hands? Not him. He's got his own ways. No," the chandler finished contentedly. "He's been there for a thousand years and he'll be there for another thousand."

Egan took the wishbone out of his pocket and looked at it again. "Will you be coming back next year?" he asked.

"Yes, indeed!" said the chandler. "I wouldn't miss it for the world. It's the best thing anywhere around. You come along, too, next year, if you like."

"Thank you," said Egan. "Maybe I'll climb up there myself, and have a look around."

"You're welcome to, as far as I'm concerned,"

said the chandler. "As long as you don't expect to find anything. Just don't take your dog along with you, that's all."

The cart jolted on into a grove of trees and Kneeknock Rise was lost to view at last.